D0833635

Cousin Markie

AND OTHER

Disasters

ACES - St. Thomas More LMC
1810 N. McDonald St.
Appleton, Wisconsin 54911

CHRISTEL KLEITSCH

Cousin Markie

AND OTHER

Disasters

ILLUSTRATED BY PAUL MEISEL

DUTTON CHILDREN'S BOOKS

NEW YORK

Text copyright © 1992 by Christel Kleitsch
Illustrations copyright © 1992 by Paul Meisel

All rights reserved. No part of this publication may be reproduced or
transmitted in any form or by any means, electronic or mechanical,
including photocopy, recording, or any information storage and retrieval
system now known or to be invented, without permission in writing from
the publisher, except by a reviewer who wishes to quote brief passages in
connection with a review written for inclusion in a magazine, newspaper,
or broadcast.

Library of Congress Cataloging-in-Publication Data

Kleitsch, Christel.
    Cousin Markie and other disasters / by Christel Kleitsch; illustrated by
Paul Meisel.–1st ed.
        p. cm.
    Summary: Ben doesn't get along with his younger cousin, and he is
certain that having him spend the weekend will ruin his plans to get a
skateboard.
    ISBN 0-525-44891-8
    [1. Cousins—Fiction. 2. Family life—Fiction.] I. Meisel, Paul, ill. II. Title.
PZ7.K67837Co 1992   91-34641
[Fic]—dc20   CIP
                                                                          AC

Published in the United States by Dutton Children's Books,
a division of Penguin Books USA Inc.
375 Hudson Street, New York, New York 10014

Designer: Sylvia Frezzolini

Printed in U.S.A.   First Edition   10 9 8 7 6 5 4 3 2 1

For Delia, with love
C.K.

Chapter 1

Ben's feet pounded along the pavement. He was on his way home from school in a big hurry.

His arch-enemy, the two-headed Swamp Monster, is hiding behind some bushes at the corner of his street. It leaps out and starts chasing him.

"Ahhh!" Ben yells and runs even faster.

He can hear the Swamp Monster coming up behind him. Closer and closer. It makes loud grunting noises as it runs.

He races up the steps to his house, slams the front door, and locks it. Outside, the Swamp Monster howls angrily and beats its hairy fists against the door.

Ben goes to the living room and opens the window. "You'll never catch me, Swamp Monster!" he yells.

"When are you going to stop playing that dumb game?" someone called.

Ben put his head out the window and looked around.

Mary Beth Armstrong was next door on her front lawn. She was walking her pet rabbit on a leash.

"When are *you* going to stop pretending that dumb rabbit is a dog?" Ben called back.

Mary Beth stuck out her tongue.

Ben bumped his head as he pulled back inside. "Ow!" he said.

He could hear Mary Beth laughing as he closed the window. He rubbed his head and made a face. That Mary Beth, she thought she was so smart. Wait until she saw him on his new skateboard tomorrow.

Ben couldn't remember a time in his life that he hadn't wanted a skateboard. He and his friend Alexander had spent endless hours hanging around the school yard watching Alexander's older brother, Graham, and his friends doing tricks on their boards. Alexander had finally gotten a board for his birthday a month ago. Since then, Ben's waiting had been almost more than he could stand. Alexander always gave him lots of turns, but it wasn't enough. Ben needed his own board.

Then this week Graham had bought himself a new skateboard. He offered Ben his old one. For only ten dollars.

Ben's chance had come at last. His only chance. He knew that his parents would never buy him a skateboard. He *had* to buy Graham's. He wanted it more than anything in the world. And today he had found a way to earn the rest of the money he needed to buy it.

Tomorrow afternoon Graham's board would be his. The weekend would be so cool. Just rolling up and down on the sidewalk in front of his house all day long. Wheelies? Curbies? Kick turns? No problem!

Ben heard the phone ring in the kitchen. His mother answered it. "Hi, Molly. What's up?" His Aunt Molly called his mother three times every day. At least.

Ben went into the kitchen. His mother smiled and wiggled her fingers "hello" at him.

His little sister, Zoe, was sitting on the floor playing with her fire truck. She looked up at him. "Beep, beep," she said, honking her nose with her finger. Zoe thought she was a car these days. If you didn't beep back, she screamed.

"Beep, beep." Ben honked his nose. "You're a monster, Zo-Zo," he said, tickling her.

Zoe giggled.

Ben took the milk out of the fridge and poured himself a glass. He wanted his mother to get off the phone. He wanted to tell her his big news.

"Mom, I'm getting my skateboard tomorrow."

"Oh, no, Ben. No skateboard, please! They're too dangerous!"

"You don't have to worry, Mom. I'll be really careful. Anyway—you promised."

"I've changed my mind." His mother starts to sniffle.

"You can't do that!"

She bursts into tears. "You'll be killed! My baby!"

Ben decided to wait until his father got home. He needed someone on his side.

Fitz, his cat, was crouched next to the refrigerator, watching the narrow space between the fridge and the wall. Every day she sat in that same spot, watching and watching.

Ben sat down on the floor beside her. "Fitzie, there's no mouse in there, you know." He scratched Fitz's favorite spot under her chin. She didn't even look at him.

"Fitzie, people are going to think that you are a very dumb cat if you don't stop doing this."

This time Fitz shot him a nasty look. She always understood everything. Ben was sure of it.

He checked behind the fridge. No mouse. Nothing but dust fluffs. "See, I told you."

"Oh, no! That's terrible," he heard his mother say.

"That's terrible" could only mean one thing. His cousin Markie was in trouble again. Like the time he got his head stuck in a bicycle wheel. Or the time he climbed out his bedroom window onto the roof to feed a baby raccoon. Or the time he ate Uncle Howard's fishing bait. A whole can of fat, slimy earthworms. Gross!

Then his mother said, "Sure, we'd be glad to have Markie for the weekend. I know Ben would—"

Oh, no! Cousin Markie for the weekend! Having to play with Markie when his family came over for supper or to visit for a few hours was bad enough—but a whole weekend!

"We'll have a great time. Bring him right over."

A great time? Sure. Markie following him around. Asking too many questions. Acting weird.

And Markie would want to ride his new skateboard. No way!

Ben was ready with his complaints the second his mother was off the phone. "Why does Markie have to come here for the weekend? He drives me crazy!"

"Don't yell, Ben," said his mother calmly. "Aunt Molly and Uncle Howard are going to a resort for their tenth anniversary. Granny was going to take care of Markie, but she came down with a bad cold. So he has to stay here."

Ben made a face. That Granny, he thought, she's pretty smart.

"Don't worry—it'll be fine; you'll see," said his mother, climbing up onto a kitchen chair. She started taking the plastic glasses with faded pictures of baseball players down from the top shelf. Then she moved all the real glasses up out of reach.

"Wash your glass when you're finished and hand it to me," she told Ben.

Ben sighed.

When Markie was a little kid, he used to bite glasses. He had taken whole chunks right out of them. It was a miracle he hadn't cut his tongue off. Aunt Molly still wouldn't let him drink out of a real glass. And she made sure everyone in the family didn't either. Ben thought it was ridiculous. He sighed again in a loud voice.

His mother looked down at him. "Ben, honey, I'm counting on you to make an effort to get along with Markie. You know I've got my hands full with Zoe—"

"I've got an idea, Mom. I'll take Zoe, and you take Markie."

His mother laughed. "It's a deal! How are you at changing diapers?"

Ben shook his head. "Gross!"

"You and Markie used to be such good play-mates when you were little. I just don't know what happened."

"He turned into a nerd, that's what happened!"

His mother's face was serious. "Ben, Markie's your cousin. Give him a chance. Remember—you're not perfect either."

Ben took a deep breath. Why couldn't his mother understand that a person his age should have the right to pick his own friends?

"What do you say, Ben?" his mother asked.

"All right, all right," he muttered.

He went out onto the back porch and sat down. His whole weekend was ruined before it even started.

There's a rustling in the bushes. Something is hiding in there. It's breathing heavily.

"Swamp Monster," Ben calls, "come and get me!"

Chapter 2

The creature crouches on a branch, looking down at Ben. Its long green head tips slowly back and forth. It never takes its eyes off him.

Slowly the creature lifts one of its front legs and starts crawling toward him. Its claws are curved and sharp as knives.

Uh-oh, thinks Ben.

Suddenly it stops. It looks like it's getting ready to leap.

Help!

The creature opens its mouth. Wide. Its fat pink tongue stretches out at Ben.

Ben closes his eyes and gets ready to die.

"Why are you closing your eyes, Ben?" Markie asked. "What are you doing?"

Ben was lying on the floor beside Markie's terrarium. He had been staring at the lizard inside for a long time. "Nothing," he said, standing up. "I was just fooling around."

"Don't you think Batman's neat?" Markie said eagerly.

Ben shrugged. "He's okay." Except for his name, he thought. Weird thing number one.

Everything about Markie was Batman. His shirt, his belt buckle, his sneakers, even his socks had bats on them. Last year it had been Ninja Turtles. And before that, Superman.

As Ben watched, Batman began licking at a drop of water on a leaf. Then he darted his head quickly from side to side, as if looking for something.

"Batman's an anole," Markie explained. "*Anolis carolinensis*—that's his real name." Markie loved telling people facts. "And did you know that if an enemy caught Batman by the tail, he could drop it off and escape? In a while, a new tail would grow."

Markie glanced at Ben to see if he was impressed. When Ben didn't say anything, he went on. "Another interesting thing is that his skin turns dark if he gets really cold."

"Maybe we could put him in the fridge for a while," Ben suggested.

Markie gave him a funny look.

"I was only kidding," Ben said.

"Oh." Markie took a little brown cricket out of a box. "Watch this, Ben."

He put the cricket into the terrarium. Before the cricket could move, Batman had it in his mouth. The cricket was wiggling its legs, trying to get away.

Batman moved his jaws a few times, and the cricket was gone. Down Batman's throat.

Ben frowned. Gross. He liked crickets. He had kept one in a box for a week once. But he had felt sorry for it, so he'd let it go.

"He was really hungry," Markie said. "I waited until I got here to feed him. So you could watch."

Thanks a lot, thought Ben. "Don't you feel kind of bad? I mean about the poor cricket?" he asked.

Markie thought about it. "If I didn't feed Batman his crickets, he would starve and die. Anyway, what do you think you're eating when you have a hamburger? A cow, right?"

Ben imagined a cow trapped inside a giant hamburger bun. He shook his head. Weird thing number two.

"Batman needs his lamp now, to keep him warm," said Markie. He set the terrarium on the desk beside Ben's bunk bed and plugged in the light. It was red. "Umm . . . Ben . . ." he said. "When we go to bed tonight, can I sleep in the top bunk? Please! I'll let you hold Batman anytime you want."

Ben never slept in the top bunk. Not since the time he had fallen out and landed on top of Fitz. But he wasn't going to tell Markie about that. "Yeah, sure, you can sleep there."

"Promise?" Markie said seriously.

Didn't Markie trust him? "Sure. I promise."

"Oh, boy!" Markie scrambled up the ladder and lay down. "Thanks a lot."

See, Mom? Ben said to himself, Markie has already done two weird things, and I'm still being nice to him.

Markie bounced around a bit. "I like the view from up here," he said happily. He looked at Ben over the edge of the bed. "Do you want to hold Batman now?"

"Maybe later," Ben said quickly. A lot later. Maybe never. Touching reptiles gave Ben the creeps.

He looked at all of Markie's things piled in the middle of the room. It was like he was moving in forever. Hey, maybe it was a trick. Maybe Markie's parents were never coming back.

Ben's mother puts her arm around him.

"Ben, honey," she says, "Markie is going to live with us from now on. He'll be sharing your room. And your clothes. And your toys. And your skateboard. Your father and I expect you to include Markie in all your games with your friends. Think of Markie as your new brother."

Ben shivered. What a nightmare! He decided to go look for his mother. He wanted to make double-sure Markie was only staying for the weekend.

Markie climbed down from the bed and followed him.

Ben stopped in place. He turned around. "Are you following me?"

Markie shrugged.

Ben sighed and kept on walking. Weird thing number three was probably coming up any second now.

Chapter 3

Ben closed his eyes and bit into his pizza slice. Melty cheese. Crisp crust. Perfect. Friday night supper was the best. It was the night his father always picked up take-out food on his way home from work.

Markie was carefully picking the green peppers, mushrooms, and olives off his pizza. He was making a real mess.

Ben remembered the fishing bait Markie had once eaten. He grinned.

Markie orders pizza: "One small pizza to go. Tomato sauce, cheese, pepperoni, and earthworms, please."

Ben's father was watching Markie, too. He looked like he was about to say something. But Ben's mother put her finger to her lips and shushed him.

"I like the pizza where we live better," Markie explained.

"No kidding," said Ben's father.

When Ben reached over to take another piece of pizza from the box, something wet and squishy hit his cheek. It was chewed-up pizza.

Zoe pointed at him and yelled, "Pee-pee! Pee-pee!"

Markie laughed. "Pee-pee?"

"She means pizza. She can't say it right," Ben told him.

Zoe took another piece of pizza out of her mouth and threw it at Markie. He ducked. It hit the wall and stuck.

"Pee-pee! Pee-pee! Pee-pee!" she yelled.

Ben and Markie laughed and shouted "Pee-pee" too.

"Cool it, you guys," said Ben's father.

"She's just a baby," said Ben.

"Yes, but you boys aren't," Ben's mother reminded them.

Zoe threw the rest of her pizza pieces onto the floor.

Only salad was left on Ben's plate now. He hated it. Rabbit food—that's what his Grandpa Nat always called it. Ben pushed it around

with his fork. When the lettuce was at the top of the plate, it looked sort of like curly hair. And the two slices of carrot could be eyes.

Now what could he use for a nose? Cucumber. Perfect.

Ben's father leaned over and looked at his plate. "My boss has hair a lot like that."

Ben laughed.

Markie picked up his glass of milk. It was a blue one with Reggie Jackson on it. "Auntie Meg?" he said. "Did my mother tell you not to give me a real glass?"

"Yeah, Mom, why do we all have to drink out of plastic glasses?" asked Ben. "They taste gross."

Ben's mother gave him a look.

"I agree," said Ben's father. "Meg, don't you think your sister is a little—"

"David, please!" Ben's mother interrupted.

"I haven't bitten a glass since I was two years old," said Markie. "I'm not a baby anymore. You just said so."

Ben's mother patted Markie's arm. "I'm sorry, honey. I promised your mother."

Markie looked down at his plate. Ben felt sorry for him. No wonder Markie was such a nerd. Aunt Molly always treated him like a baby.

His own mom wasn't much better. She was always bothering Ben to be careful. He had gotten a two-wheeler a whole year later than all his friends because of her worrying. And it had taken him hours of nagging and begging to get her to agree to let him get a skateboard. He even had to cry once.

"Auntie Meg, can I get my allowance now?" said Markie, his mouth full of salad. "I always get it at suppertime on Fridays."

"Can I have mine, too?" Ben asked.

Ben's father took out his wallet. "Don't spend it all in one place," he said, handing Markie and Ben a dollar each.

One dollar, plus the four dollars I've already got saved, makes five, thought Ben. Just five to go and I get the skateboard.

Markie looked at the money .in his hand. "Didn't you know I get two dollars allowance, Uncle David?"

"Two dollars!" Ben's father said.

"Two!" exclaimed Ben.

His mother nodded. "Give them both two, David."

"All right," said his father. "But just this one time."

Ben started thinking about Markie being a whole year younger and getting more allowance than he did. And how unfair that was. And how he could use one dollar more every week.

He looked over at his father.

His father shook his head. "Sorry, Ben. But you're not due for a raise until your birthday."

It drove Ben crazy how his parents could read his mind sometimes.

It was time to tell them his big news. Ben took a nervous breath. He hoped his mother wouldn't give him any trouble.

He forced his face into a big smile and looked up from his plate. "Guess what? I got a job raking the Peabodys' leaves tomorrow morning. They're paying me five dollars. Because their yard is so big and there are so many trees."

"Five dollars! That's very generous pay," said his mother.

"Make sure you do a good job," his father added.

"And guess what else?" Ben said, keeping his voice bright and cheerful. "Alexander's brother, Graham, is selling me his old skateboard. Only ten dollars. I'll get it tomorrow." Then he flashed another big smile and waited.

He glanced over at his mother. Sure enough, she was frowning.

"David, are you sure it's a good idea for Ben to have a skateboard? I've been thinking it over—"

"Mom!" groaned Ben.

"My parents won't let me get one either," Markie piped up.

"Who cares?" Ben snapped at him. "And anyway, I *am* getting one. Right, Dad?"

"Ben!" said his mother sharply.

Markie didn't look at Ben. He just kept on talking. "This kid on our street broke his arm in sixteen places when he fell off his skateboard."

Shut up, Markie! Ben thought.

Ben's father laughed. "That's a lot of places, Markie."

Ben was starting to panic. He had to get them to stop talking about skateboards before Markie ruined everything.

"Hey!" he said. "Zo-Zo's putting a mushroom up her nose."

Zoe shook her head. "Me *not!*" she said. "Me *not!*"

His parents kept on talking. "Meg, I'm sure with elbow and kneepads Ben will be just fine," said his father. He turned to Ben with a wink. "Say, did your mother tell you yet where we're going on Sunday?"

"Where, Mom?" Ben gave his father a grateful smile.

"Frontier Town," said his mother. "Aunt Molly and Uncle Howard's treat for you boys."

"All right!" said Ben. Frontier Town was a Wild West theme park. There were rides and games and people dressed up in old-fashioned clothes. He moved the green pepper on his plate to make a smiling face. This weekend might not turn out to be so bad, after all—a skateboard *and* Frontier Town.

"I brought all my cowboy clothes," Markie announced proudly.

"Cowboy clothes are for babies," Ben said under his breath.

His parents were talking and didn't hear him.

Markie did, though. He frowned and looked away.

Chapter 4

After supper Ben picked up the phone and dialed Alexander's number.

Alexander answered. "Hi, Ben. Is your mom letting you get Graham's skateboard?"

"Yes!" said Ben. "I'll pick it up tomorrow."

"Cool! Do you want to talk to Graham? I'll get him." Alexander put the phone down.

Ben waited. And waited. What was Alexander doing? He had a bad habit of leaving Ben waiting on the phone for a long time. Once he had even taken a bath.

There were golf balls lying all over the living room floor. Ben's father had his golf clubs out and was practicing his putting. He had set up a putting course of paper cups around the furniture. And he was listening to his old Electric Prunes record.

Ben knew it drove his mother crazy when

his father golfed in the living room. He had already broken a lamp and a mirror. She didn't like the Electric Prunes that much either.

Zoe was sitting behind the couch, stuffing golf balls into her diaper. She looked like she was having fun. Ben grinned. He wondered whether her diaper was clean.

Alexander came back on the line. "Hi, Ben. Graham won't come to the phone. He's watching TV."

"Okay. Just tell him I'll come over with the money around lunch."

"Cool," said Alexander. "Bye."

Suddenly there was a lot of yelling. Ben's parents had noticed Zoe. Ben's father took her upstairs to change her.

Ben heard Fitz meowing at the back door. He went to let her in.

"You might as well put Fitzie and all her stuff down in the basement now," his mother said.

"What?" said Ben. "Why?"

"Markie is allergic to cats, remember? Fitz can't sleep with you for a couple of nights."

"But"—Ben thought fast—"what about the mice? They come out at night. To eat our stuff."

His mother looked puzzled. "Mice?"

"You know, the ones behind the fridge."

She laughed. "Are you kidding? The only mice around here are in that crazy cat's head."

"Markie belongs in the basement, not Fitz!" Ben yelled.

"Stop it, Ben. Markie might hear you," said his mother. "Fitz will survive. Millions of cats the world over sleep in basements."

Ben dragged Fitz's bowls and her sleeping basket into the basement.

Fitz walked around, neatly sniffing at the boxes and rolled-up carpets.

Poor Fitz, thought Ben. She probably won't be able to sleep a wink down here. She'll probably be meowing for me all night. He gave her a big hug. "Sorry, Fitzie, you old mouser."

Fitz licked his hand with her sandpaper tongue. Then she went over to her basket, curled up, and closed her eyes.

Ben couldn't believe it. She was asleep. Some pal!

By the time Ben got to his room, he was feeling crabby.

Markie was already lying in the top bunk. He was wearing Batman pajamas. Of course.

"I changed my mind," Ben told him. "You can't sleep in the top bunk."

Markie looked down. "But you promised! It's not fair."

"I don't care. It's my bed. My room. My house," said Ben.

Markie climbed slowly down the ladder. "I'll tell your mother."

"Snitcher!" Ben said.

Markie walked to the door of the bedroom. He put his hand on the doorknob. Then he stopped and looked back at Ben.

Ben did not want to get in trouble with his mother. But he wasn't going to back down either. If he couldn't sleep with Fitzie, Markie couldn't sleep in the top bunk.

Markie thought a moment. Then he let go of the doorknob. "I'm not a snitcher!" he said loudly.

He went over and opened his suitcase. He

took out a purple plastic dinosaur. He stared at Ben as he walked back to the bed, daring him to say something mean about the dinosaur. Ben decided not to.

Then Markie crawled into the bottom bunk and pulled the covers over his head. Ben could hear him whispering to the dinosaur.

Ben put on his pajamas and climbed up the ladder to the top bunk. As soon as he lay down, he realized that he had been dumb. Very, very dumb. He couldn't sleep up here! He just knew that the moment he fell asleep, he would roll over and go crashing down to the floor. He could picture himself lying in the hospital, both arms and both legs in huge casts. It would be a year before he could ride the skateboard.

The house sounded very still. Outside the wind rustled through the dry leaves on the tree by his window. A dog barked far away. Ben snuggled farther down under his blanket. He missed Fitzie curled up by his feet.

"Hey, Markie," he whispered, "do you want to switch beds?"

Markie didn't answer.

Ben leaned over the edge of his bunk. Markie slept the way Zoe did, with his rear end sticking up in the air. He had the purple dinosaur clutched tightly under his arm. Without his glasses on, he looked like a little kid.

Ben dragged his blanket and pillow down the ladder. He curled up on the carpet.

"Good night, Markie," he whispered.

Chapter 5

Ben opened one eye. Markie was lying beside him on the floor, watching him. Breathing on him.

Ben closed his eye again. "What do you want?"

"Did you fall out of bed?" Markie asked.

"No."

"Then why are you down here?"

Ben thought fast. "I must have sleepwalked."

"Oh." Markie looked confused. Then he said, "Is it okay if I play with your Lego blocks, Ben?"

Ben nodded. He looked at his watch. Seven-thirty. Too early to go to the Peabodys' to rake their leaves. He crawled into the bottom bunk and pretended to snore.

Markie got out the Lego bin and dumped the pieces noisily onto the floor.

"Not in here, Markie!" snapped Ben from

under the covers. "Take it to the living room."

"Okay, okay," said Markie. "You don't have to yell." He gathered up the Lego pieces and carried the bin out of the room.

Ben closed his eyes, but no matter how hard he tried, he couldn't go back to sleep. He kept thinking about his skateboard. It was hard to believe that he was really going to get it. Today.

He looked into Markie's terrarium. Batman was sitting on a branch. There was a cricket hiding under a leaf in the corner. "Good luck, cricket," Ben said.

Batman nodded his head a few times. Then he leaped onto the glass wall of the terrarium. The little suckers on the bottoms of his toes were sticking to the glass.

Cool, thought Ben. I wish I could do that.

The kids in Ben's class are filing into the room.

"Wow, look at that!" cries Alexander and points up.

Everyone gasps. It's Ben, Lizard Boy. He's walking up the classroom wall. He grins down at them.

"Ben Eliot, you come down from there!" says his teacher, Mrs. Dickie, looking pale.

Ben lashes out his long, sticky tongue and snatches a piece of chalk out of her hand. She screams and faints.

Vrrrmm. The car started in the driveway. That meant his mother was driving Zoe to her baby gym class. Then he heard his father singing in the shower. It was time to head over to the Peabodys'.

Ben got dressed and went to the kitchen. A box of Honey Puffys was on the table. Empty. Not even any cereal dust left in the bottom. That Markie!

Ben made himself a big peanut butter–and-banana-and-raisin sandwich and went out on the back deck. Markie had taken some clubs from Ben's father's golf bag. He was trying to hit the ball across the backyard. He was pretty good, too.

Mary Beth Armstrong was sitting on top of the fence between her yard and Ben's. She was petting her rabbit.

"You should be using the putter, kid," she told Markie.

"Mind your own beeswax, Mary Beth," Ben said. Mary Beth always thought she knew everything about everything.

She stuck out her tongue. "The Swamp Monster will get you."

Ben, Lizard Boy, lashes out his tongue across the yard. He snatches the rabbit out of Mary Beth's arms. She screams and faints.

"Which one is the putter, Ben?" Markie asked.

"It's the one with the little end. The flat one."

Markie held it up and Ben nodded.

Ben could hear his father still singing in the shower. His father did not like anyone touching his golf stuff. "Markie, you better put—" he started to say.

"Watch this, Ben." Markie lifted the golf club way over his shoulder just like Greg Norman, the golf champ.

"Markie! Don't!" Ben yelled.

Markie swung the club. The ball lifted up into the air. Ben couldn't believe his eyes. What a hit!

CRASH!! The ball smashed right through the bathroom window.

Ben's father stopped singing. He started yelling. He stuck his nose out through the broken window and kept on yelling. Ben didn't know his father knew so many of those words.

Mary Beth was laughing so hard she fell off the fence, taking her rabbit with her.

A second later his father was at the back door with a towel around his middle. He was dripping wet, and he had a red spot on his forehead. The rest of his face looked kind of red, too. This is where Markie dies, thought Ben. His father had a terrible temper.

Markie looked like he was going to cry. "Uncle David, does this mean we're not going to Frontier Town?" he asked.

Ben's father didn't answer. He stormed back into the house, slamming the door so hard that Ben was sure the rest of the windows in the house would break, too.

Ben was amazed. Just a door slam? No threats? No throwing things?

Mary Beth's head popped up over the fence. "Kid, that was an amazing shot."

"Shut up!" said Ben.

Ben and Markie stood around miserably until Ben's father came back out of the house. He was dressed. He had also calmed down. Sort of.

"All right, you two jokers," he said, "listen up. Number one, you clean up the glass and help me take that window out. Number two, you come with me to the hardware store to get new glass. And number three, you contribute your allowances to the cost of the new window."

Markie just kept nodding the whole time Ben's father was talking. He looked scared.

"But, Dad—" said Ben.

"No *buts!*" his father said sternly.

"But, Dad—" said Ben again. He wanted to say that it wasn't his fault that Markie broke the window. He wanted to say that he had promised to rake the Peabodys' leaves this morning. He wanted to say that he needed his allowance to buy the skateboard.

"NO *BUTS!!*" His father's face was starting to get red again.

Ben closed his mouth. He decided to keep it closed.

Chapter 6

It was almost two o'clock in the afternoon before the window was finally fixed. Ben was just about jumping out of his skin, he was so eager to get over to the Peabodys' house. The whole time, he had been imagining terrible things happening.

MYSTERIOUS CYCLONE HITS

Saturday morning, a mysterious cyclone descended on the yard of Mr. and Mrs. Peabody, 25 Butternut Street. It picked up the retired couple, their house, and their entire yard with all the fallen leaves and carried them off into outer space. "I haven't seen anything like this since *The Wizard of Oz*," said Professor Barometer of the Weather Office.

Markie followed Ben out of the house. "Can I help you, Ben?" he asked. "I really like raking leaves. You won't have to pay me either."

Ben nodded. He figured it was the least Markie could do for getting him in trouble. And making him lose out on his skateboard for this weekend. After this job, he would still have only nine dollars.

When they got to the Peabodys' house, there were six humongous garbage bags sitting by the curb. And no leaves in the yard.

"Oh, no!" Ben groaned. His stomach suddenly felt all knotted. "What's going on?" He knocked at the front door.

Mrs. Peabody opened it. "Hello, boys," she said softly. "What can I do for you?" Mrs. Peabody matched her voice perfectly. She was the tiniest, skinniest person Ben had ever seen.

Ben had to swallow before he could speak. The words still came out all crumply. "Mrs. Peabody, yesterday you said I could rake your leaves. Remember? For five dollars."

"Oh, was that you, dear?" Mrs. Peabody looked confused. "When you didn't come this morning, we thought you had forgotten. Mr. Peabody gave the job to a little girl."

Ben couldn't say anything. His skateboard was slipping further and further away. He felt like crying.

"I know," said Mrs. Peabody brightly. "You could shovel our walk when it snows. Yes, come back on the first snowy day and the job will be yours. I promise." And she winked at Ben and closed the door.

Ben turned and walked away. Markie followed. After a minute, Markie said softly, "It wasn't very nice of them to—"

Ben was so angry he felt like exploding. "Shut up, Markie, okay?" he yelled. "It's all your fault! You broke the window and made me late. You got me in trouble, and I didn't even do anything. Now I'll never get my skateboard. You are such a nerd. Everything is your *stupid* fault!"

Ben turned and kept on walking fast. Suddenly he felt a hard shove from behind. He almost fell forward onto the sidewalk. "Hey! What's—"

It was Markie.

"I *hate* you!" Markie yelled. "I *hate* you! It's

not my fault you lost your job—it's *your* fault. You should have telephoned the people to tell them you were going to be late."

Ben stared. Markie's eyes were wild, and his cheeks were red. Ben didn't know what to say.

"Every time I come to your house you're always mean to me," Markie went on. "You're nothing but a rotten bully. Even my mommy and daddy say you are."

A bully?

"I wish I wasn't your cousin so I would never have to play with you ever again!" Markie turned and ran down the street toward Ben's house.

Ben let out a deep breath. Markie had never gotten mad at him like this before.

And no one had ever called him a bully in his whole life. A bully was Allan Topping, who had picked on Ben every day in the school yard when he was in first grade. A bully was a mean person.

I'm not a bully, Ben thought.

Am I?

Chapter 7

It was Sunday morning. Ben, his father, and Zoe were sitting in the car, ready to go to Frontier Town. They were waiting for Ben's mother and Markie.

Ben's father looked at his watch. "Seventeen minutes—and counting."

"Wouldn't it be funny if we just left without them?" Ben was not looking forward to spending another day with Markie. Since their fight yesterday, Markie had not spoken to him. Not one word. Even when Ben had tried to be nice and offered him the top bunk, Markie just ignored him.

Ben kept thinking about what Markie had said, about him being a bully. The idea of his Aunt Molly and Uncle Howard and Markie talking about him like that when he wasn't around made him embarrassed.

Ben looked over at his father. Did his father think he was a bully, too? Ben didn't think so, but he was afraid to ask. Maybe Markie was making the whole thing up. Maybe his aunt and uncle hadn't ever called him a bully. Ben didn't know what to think.

"I'm going to go nuts back here," his father said. He shifted his knees uncomfortably.

Ben's father had to ride in the backseat because of Markie. Markie was famous for getting carsick. Ben's mother had once explained that there was something wrong with the middle of Markie's ear or his brain or something—Ben couldn't exactly remember.

Mary Beth Armstrong came slamming out her front door. She put her rabbit down on the lawn. She held a carrot to the rabbit's nose, and then she threw it a little way ahead. "Fetch, Snuffy," she said.

Ben shook his head. Mary Beth had finally gone crazy.

The rabbit hopped ahead and started to nibble the carrot. "No, Snuffy! Fetch—don't eat." Mary Beth grabbed the carrot away.

Ben grinned. Her rabbit was a lot smarter than she was.

Zoe started yelling. Ben handed her another breadstick—her fifth one. It was the only way they could keep her quiet.

Everything in the backseat was covered with crumbs. Ben's father looked at it gloomily. He worried a lot about the upholstery. "Twenty-one minutes," he said, "and counting."

A few minutes later, the front door of the house opened. Markie came out on the porch. He was wearing a cowboy hat, a string tie, a cowboy shirt, cowboy pants with fringes down the legs, and plastic cowboy boots. A coiled-up lasso hung over his shoulder.

Ben shook his head. Markie looked dumb, really dumb. Ben glanced over at Mary Beth Armstrong. He hoped that she wouldn't see Markie.

Good. She was still bothering her rabbit.

"Well, howdy, pardner!" said Ben's father, smiling. "What took you so long?"

"We had a little problem with Markie's out-fit," said Ben's mother.

As Markie got closer to the car, Ben could see that his eyes were red from crying.

"My cowboy guns. I need them," Markie said. "Please, Uncle David?"

Ben's father shook his head. "Sorry."

Ben knew exactly how Markie felt. No toy guns. That was his family's dumb rule.

"Hey, kid!" Mary Beth yelled.

Uh-oh, she had seen Markie.

"Cool cowboy clothes, dude!" she said.

Markie perked up. "Thanks!"

Ben couldn't believe it. Mary Beth and Markie were *both* double-weird.

"Auntie Meg, can I ride in the backseat with Zoe?" said Markie. "Please?"

Not "Zoe and Ben," thought Ben. Just Zoe. Who am I, the Invisible Man?

Ben's mother started the car. "Sure, Markie, let's give it a try. But let us know right away if you start feeling sick, okay?"

Markie nodded.

"Hot diggety!" said Ben's father. He unfolded himself and got into the front of the car.

Ben slumped down in his seat. He hoped

nothing gross would happen. Sometimes his mom was too nice. She probably felt badly about Markie and his guns.

Markie honked his nose at Zoe. "Beep, beep," he said.

Zoe laughed. "Beep! Beep!" she answered.

Markie rode with his head up, sniffing the air from the window. He looked just like Alexander's dog, Pavlov, Ben thought.

"Are we almost there?" Markie asked.

"We've only gone ten blocks," Ben's father said.

Ben looked at Markie. He was green. Ben had never seen anyone turn that color. "Stop the car, Mom!" he yelled.

Markie just made it out of the car before he tossed his cookies. Double-gross, thought Ben.

"All right, Markie, in the front," said Ben's father grimly.

Markie didn't argue. He just looked miserable.

After a while, Ben heard quiet snoring beside him. Zoe had fallen asleep in her car seat.

The sun was shining hot through the car

window. It made Ben feel sleepy, too. He leaned his head back on the seat and closed his eyes. He thought about the other times he had gone to Frontier Town.

There was a ride called Ghost Town. It was like a Halloween haunted house, only much bigger. Ben liked the scary things that jumped out from behind doors and fences.

The logjam ride was cool, too. You felt just like you were riding a giant skateboard over a waterfall. *Whoosh!*

Ben sighed. His skateboard. How was he ever going to get it now? If he didn't come up with the money soon, Graham might sell it to someone else.

He thought about the outlaws in Frontier Town who held up the stagecoach ride. The sheriff always arrived and chased them, but the outlaws never got caught. Every time they managed to get away with the money.

Maybe I could try it, too, Ben thought. Just once.

Ben Eliot, Fearless Outlaw, swaggers boldy into the Frontier Town Bank. He steps up to a window. *"Stick 'em up!"* he snarls to the teller. *"Hand over six dollars."*

The teller looks scared. "Sure, mister," he says. "Just don't shoot."

"Oh, don't worry," says Ben. "My mom and dad won't let me play with guns."

Ben smiled. Some outlaw he'd make.

The car went over a bump. He opened his eyes. Markie was telling his mother some boring facts about life in the Wild West.

Ben sighed and closed his eyes again. Markie would probably cry in Ghost Town. Or be sick on the logjam ride. How could anyone be friends with a kid like Markie?

Chapter 8

Ben stood reading the names on the Wanted posters in the stagecoach office. Billy the Kid. Cole Younger. Frank and Jesse James. The Clanton brothers.

The Clantons looked like the outlaws who always robbed the stagecoach. They both had bushy beards and big bandannas around their necks. WANTED DEAD OR ALIVE, the poster said. TWO HUNDRED DOLLARS REWARD.

Markie came and stood behind Ben. He was reading the Wanted posters, too.

"All aboard!" shouted the stagecoach driver outside.

Ben headed for the door, but Markie was still staring at the poster of the Clantons.

"Come on, Markie, time to go," called Ben's father.

Ben handed the driver his ticket and climbed

into the stagecoach. He sat down next to the window.

Then Markie climbed in. He went over to the window on the other side of the stagecoach and sat down.

A little girl with curly red hair sat next to Ben. Her mother asked Ben to keep an eye on her during the ride. The little girl smiled at Ben.

Ben waved to his mother and father and Zoe as the stagecoach started off.

"Have fun," called his mother.

"Ha pun," echoed Zoe.

The stagecoach drove along a bumpy road. Dust blew in through the open windows. Markie started sneezing, over and over. All the kids looked at him.

Suddenly two men on horseback rode up alongside the stagecoach.

Bang! Bang-bang!

It was the outlaws! They had come to rob the stagecoach!

"Don't worry," Ben whispered to the little girl beside him, "it's just pretend."

She looked at Ben with a grin. "I know," she said. "It's *so* neat!"

The stagecoach stopped. "Reach for the sky," someone shouted.

Ben looked out through the window. The two outlaws jumped off their horses. They kept yelling at the stagecoach driver to put up his hands and not move. With their hats pulled low over their eyes and bandannas tied over their mouths and noses, the outlaws looked tough and scary, even to Ben.

One of the outlaws climbed up on top of the stagecoach where the driver was sitting. The strongbox with the money was hidden under the driver's seat.

The other outlaw leaned in the window of the stagecoach. "Keep quiet and sit tight. All we want is the money," he growled.

"He's a big meany!" whispered the little girl next to Ben.

He patted her shoulder. "It's okay," he said.

Ben glanced over at Markie to see if he was all right, but Markie was busy doing something with his lasso.

Ben heard the strongbox land on the ground with a thump, right beside the stagecoach. He watched as the two outlaws started smashing at the lock with the butts of their guns.

"What are they doing now?" Ben heard Markie ask.

"They're opening the strongbox." As Ben turned to answer, he noticed that Markie was crouching on the floor of the stagecoach. Ben figured he better say something. "The outlaws won't hurt you, Markie. It's only pretend."

Markie looked up at Ben. "Shhh!" he whispered. "You be my lookout."

Ben was confused. "What?"

Markie didn't answer. He was opening the door on his side of the stagecoach.

"What are you doing, Markie?" Ben whispered.

But Markie was already gone.

Ben leaned out the stagecoach window. The outlaws had broken the lock and were opening the strongbox.

Then he saw Markie sneak over to where the outlaws' horses were tied to a tree. Markie dashed around to the horses' heads. Ben couldn't see what he was doing there because the horses kept moving in the way.

Suddenly Ben heard another horse galloping toward them. It was the sheriff.

The outlaws scrambled to stuff the rest of the money into their saddlebags.

"Markie! Hurry up!" Ben yelled.

Markie came running toward the stagecoach. Ben opened the door and helped him in.

"What were you doing?" Ben asked him.

Markie looked through the window. "Shhh," he said, "you'll see."

The outlaws grabbed the saddlebags and raced over to leap on their horses. But instead of galloping off, the horses just pranced around and around in one spot. The outlaws were yelling at each other.

"What's going on?" asked Ben. "What are they doing?"

Markie was bouncing up and down. "It worked! It worked! I tied the horses' reins together with my lasso. They can't get away!"

The sheriff rode up in a swirl of dust. "Stick 'em high!" he shouted. "I got you covered!"

The outlaws raised their hands in the air.

Ben couldn't believe it. The outlaws were captured. And Markie had done it. *His* cousin Markie!

All the kids in the stagecoach were excited. "Yay!" yelled the little girl beside Ben. Everyone clapped for Markie.

Ben did, too. He hoped Markie noticed.

Chapter 9

Sheriff Watson had the biggest mustache Ben had ever seen. It stuck out wide on both sides of his face with little curls on the ends. And it moved up and down when he talked. Ben couldn't stop watching it.

Ben and his family and Markie were all in the sheriff's office. He had invited them over for a special tour.

The sheriff reached out and pulled the poster of the Clanton brothers off the wall. "Here, keep this for a souvenir, young fellow," he said, handing it to Markie. "Thanks to you, I won't be needing it anymore."

Markie grinned proudly. He rolled the poster up and held it tightly in his hand.

"I've been trying to capture those gunslingers eight times a day for nearly three years," the sheriff told Ben's parents with a wink.

"And they got away on me every time. You should be mighty proud of this young fellow."

"He's pretty smart, all right," said Ben's mother. "And he did it without guns."

The sheriff went to his desk. He opened a drawer and reached in for something. "Just to show my appreciation, Markie, I'd like to give you this."

A deputy badge. Shiny silver. Shaped like a star. The real thing. Cool! Ben said to himself.

The sheriff pinned the badge to Markie's shirt. Then he shook his hand. "Congratulations, Deputy Markie."

Markie's ears turned all red. He looked down at his badge. "Thanks!"

"That's great, Markie," said Ben's father.

Markie had an enormous grin on his face. He looked like he would burst with happiness. Ben felt happy for him, too. He wanted to go over to look at Markie's badge more closely, but he didn't. He wasn't sure whether Markie was still angry with him or not.

Sheriff Watson rubbed his hands together. "Well, now, I think this calls for some sarsaparilla pop. It's not every day I get myself a new deputy."

He got out a big bottle and some Frontier Town glasses.

"Umm . . . Sheriff . . ." Markie said. "My cousin Ben should have a deputy badge, too. He helped me capture the outlaws."

Ben stared at Markie. He couldn't figure him out. One minute Markie wouldn't even speak to him; now he was being nice. Too nice. Ben knew that he didn't really deserve a badge. Markie had done it all by himself.

Ben shook his head. "I was only the lookout, Sheriff. I didn't do anything."

"Is that so?" said the sheriff. "Well, let me tell you, young fellow, everybody is important in a dangerous operation like this. My life has been saved many times by the sharp eyes of a dependable lookout. Anyway, with all these gunslingers around here, I could use an extra deputy."

Ben held very still as Sheriff Watson pinned on the deputy badge. "Thanks, Sheriff!" he said. Ben touched his badge. It felt heavy hanging on his shirt. Like a real deputy badge, not like a toy at all. He glanced over at Markie and smiled. Markie smiled back.

Zoe pointed to Ben's badge. "Ta! Ta!" she yelled.

"Yes, Zoe, star, star," Ben said, smiling.

"Sheriff?" Markie asked. "When do we get the reward money?"

The sheriff looked puzzled. "Reward money?"

Markie held out the poster. "Like it says here—two hundred dollars reward. One hundred dollars each for Ben and me."

One hundred dollars! Ben had forgotten all about the reward money. Deputy badges were one thing, but could Markie really get them all that money, too? All right! he thought. Skateboard, here I come.

"Markie, I don't think—" said Ben's mother.

"Two hundred dollars?" The sheriff didn't seem to know what to say. He stared at the poster and scratched his head. Ben realized that there was really no reward money.

"Let's not forget it was just a ride," said Ben's father. "You've already—"

"Sorry, boys," said Sheriff Watson. He was

smiling. Like he had just gotten a good idea. "Deputies don't get rewards. It's a strict rule."

"Well, of course not," said Ben's mother.

"But we weren't deputies when we captured the outlaws," Markie reminded the sheriff.

"Well, that's true. . . ." The sheriff started to look worried again.

"How about if I give you boys a little reward myself?" Ben's father suggested. "Let's say you get back the allowance you lost for breaking the window. Okay?"

"And I'll even throw in the Frontier Town glasses—free," said the sheriff, giving Ben's father a grateful look. "Well, now that's settled, let's see about these drinks." He poured everyone a big drink of sarsaparilla.

Markie still looked unhappy. "But I wanted Ben to get the money for his skateboard," he said. "Now he still won't have enough."

"Markie!" said Ben's mother. "That was so kind of you. Wasn't it, Ben?"

Ben nodded slowly. He knew that his mother was right. Markie *was* being kind. Kinder than me, he thought, remembering the things he had done to Markie that weekend.

Markie was staring at the glasses of sarsaparilla on Sheriff Watson's desk. Then he looked at Ben's mother.

She frowned and turned to say something to the sheriff.

Ben thought fast. He couldn't let his mother embarrass Markie in front of the sheriff by making him drink out of a plastic glass. "Remember, Mom," he said. "Markie's a deputy now."

"You're right," she said. She smiled and picked up her glass. "Drink up, Markie."

Markie grinned broadly and drank his pop. When he put the glass down, it was empty. And there were no bites taken out of it. "See, Auntie Meg," he said, "you don't have to worry about me."

Suddenly Sheriff Watson yelled out, "Hey!!!"

Everyone looked down. Zoe was sitting on the floor. She was pouring her drink into the sheriff's boot.

They all laughed. Zoe looked up and grinned.

Ben shook his head. What a monster!

He could see it now. A new poster up on the
sheriff's wall:

Chapter 10

All of Markie's stuff was piled in the front hall.

Ben went over to the terrarium. He tapped softly on the glass. Batman turned to look at him and moved his head up and down. Ben wiggled his fingers. "Bye, Batman."

Ben spotted Zoe's fire truck on the floor. He nudged it with his foot. It rolled forward.

He stepped on top of the fire truck with one foot and used the other foot to push himself along.

Clack . . . clack . . . clack . . . Ben Eliot, Skateboard Whiz, is rolling along the sidewalk.

He puts both feet on the board and holds his arms out to balance himself.

Clackity. Clackity. Clackity! Clackity! He's roaring down the hill, faster and faster. Oh, no, the pavement's getting really rough!

Ben begins to tip wildly.

Is he going to make it!?!!

The skateboard flips, and he tumbles onto the ground.

"Wipeout!" he yells.

Wipeout is right, Ben thought, setting the fire truck back onto its wheels again. For this weekend, anyway. But now he had six dollars, and if he saved every penny of his allowance, it would take four more weeks. Less, if he found another job. He was going to get Graham's skateboard yet. Somehow.

Ben went into the kitchen. Markie was standing beside the fridge. He was watching the space between the fridge and the wall. When he noticed Ben, he put his finger to his lips. "Shhh!"

Ben tiptoed closer and peered over Markie's shoulder. Nothing. "What did you see?" he whispered.

"I'm not sure," whispered Markie, "but I think it was a mouse."

"I knew it!" yelled Ben. "I knew there was a mouse! Hurray for Fitzie the mouser!"

He ran to the basement door and called down the stairs. "Fitzie, come quick! That mouse is back!"

Fitz shot past his legs and went over to the fridge. She crouched by the space and watched.

"I think you scared it away when you yelled," said Markie.

"It will be back," said Ben. "And Fitzie will be waiting." He leaned down and scratched Fitz's head. "Right, Fitzie?"

Markie sat on the floor beside Fitz and started to pet her. "I'm sorry about Fitzie having to sleep in the basement while I was here. I like her. It's just that I'm allergic."

"I know," said Ben. "It's okay."

Markie sneezed. Then he sneezed again. And again.

Ben laughed. "I believe you, I believe you."

Markie laughed, too. "I hope you get your skateboard soon, Ben," he said.

"I'll think of something. I phoned Graham and made him promise not to sell it to anybody else." Ben touched the deputy badge on his shirt. "Thanks for trying to get me the money."

"That's okay," said Markie.

"I thought you were mad at me."

"I was," said Markie. "I was *really* mad." He grinned. "But then I decided to give you another chance. My mommy says cousins are for your whole life."

"My mom is always saying stuff like that, too." Ben paused. "Markie . . . umm . . ." This wasn't easy. ". . . I'm sorry I yelled at you yesterday about losing the job raking leaves."

Markie shrugged. "That's okay."

Ben took a deep breath. He had to say it. "You called me a bully."

Markie shook his head. "I didn't mean it, Ben," he said. "Sorry. Sometimes you do rotten things to me like not letting me sleep in the top bunk, but I don't—"

"And your parents don't think I'm a bully either?" Ben interrupted.

Markie looked surprised. "No, they like you."

Suddenly Ben felt like giving Markie a hug. So he did.

Markie smiled at him. "Let's go out on the front porch and wait for my mommy and daddy."

As Ben and Markie were sitting down on the porch steps, Ben heard a rustling in the bushes beside him. Something was hiding in there. *The two-headed Swamp Monster?*

Ben climbed down from the steps. He moved aside some branches and peered into the bushes. A white rabbit looked back at him. It blinked twice and then wiggled its pink nose.

"It's Snuffy!" he told Markie. "Mary Beth's rabbit."

Markie crawled into the bushes to get the rabbit. Then he sat on the grass with the rabbit in his lap and patted it.

Ben patted it, too. "I'm positive it's Snuffy," he said. "He's pretty cute up close."

"He must have run away," Markie said.

Ben grinned. "Can you blame him?"

Markie laughed. "We better take him back."

"You do it," Ben said. "You caught him."

Markie shook his head. "No way! You do it. She's your neighbor."

Ben sighed. "All right, let's both do it."

Mary Beth answered the doorbell. "You found him!" she cried. "Oh, thank you!" She

took Snuffy out of Markie's arms and hugged him tight. "Oh, you naughty Snuffy," she said, kissing him on the nose. "Don't you ever run away again."

"He was in Ben's bushes," Markie said.

"He was probably on his way home," said Mary Beth. "Weren't you, Snuffy?" She kissed him again.

Ben looked at Markie and rolled his eyes.

Mary Beth carried Snuffy over to the stairs in the hallway. "Mommy, guess what?" she yelled up. "Ben and his cousin found Snuffy."

"That's great!" called her mother. "Thanks, boys. Remember to give them the reward, honey."

"Reward?" said Ben.

"Didn't you see my posters?" Mary Beth told him. "There's a reward for finding Snuffy." She yelled up the stairs again. "I'll give them six each, okay, Mommy?"

"That's fine," her mother called.

"I'll be right back," said Mary Beth. And she went into the kitchen.

Ben and Markie looked at each other and

grinned. It was too good to be true. "Six dollars!" Markie said. "Wow!"

"Skateboard, here I come!" Ben said.

Mary Beth came out of the kitchen carrying two plates of chocolate-chip cookies. "The reward was a dozen cookies, so you each get six," she explained.

"Cookies?!?" said Ben and Markie together.

Mary Beth narrowed her eyes. "What's wrong? Don't you guys want my mother's cookies?"

"Sure we want them," Markie said, taking his pile of cookies off the plate. "Thanks."

Ben swallowed his disappointment and took his cookies, too.

"Thanks for finding Snuffy," Mary Beth called as Ben and Markie walked back to Ben's house.

"No problem," said Markie.

Ben went into the house and came out with the two Frontier Town glasses full of milk. He and Markie sat on the front steps happily munching their cookies and drinking milk together. Ben remembered how upset he had been about Markie coming for the weekend. And how mad he always got about the weird things Markie did.

But the weirdest thing of all, Ben thought, is Markie and me getting to be friends.

Ben turned to Markie. "Your parents are late."

Markie rolled his eyes. "Parents are *always* late."

"Do you want to do something?" Ben asked.

"Sure," said Markie. He smiled. "How about playing golf?"

And they both laughed.

ACES - St. Thomas More LMC
1810 N. McDonald St.
Appleton, Wisconsin 54911